J. DAVID TOWNSEND

Illustrated by Trina Hyman

# The Five Trials of the Pansy Bed

1 9 6 7

HOUGHTON MIFFLIN COMPANY BOSTON

J. David Townsend
has also written
THE CATS STAND ACCUSED

*First Printing*  w

# CONTENTS

**To Paul,**
my grandson,
who gave the book its title.

## Alice Plants Her Pansies

*Alice* watched her father put his garden tools away in a corner of the garage. She counted them. There were four — the hoe, the rake, the spade, and the shovel. Alice had a hoe and rake of her own, but she liked Daddy's tools better. Maybe because they were brighter and cleaner than hers. They had been new the spring before.

Mr. Taylor's face looked sad and his voice sounded discouraged when he spoke. "There!

2

I'm through with them," he said. "I'll never try to grow flowers here again."

"Why, Daddy?" Alice asked.

"Because I never have any luck with them. Nothing seems to want to grow for me."

"Maybe if you tried just once more," Alice said timidly.

"No—I'm through. For three years I've planted the best seeds and bulbs. And, goodness knows, I've fertilized them and watered them and kept them free of weeds."

"What does fer-til-ized mean, Daddy?"

"Oh, that's when you put something—like rich soil or minerals—in the ground for the plants to eat. You see, the earth in our yard is poor and sandy, and nothing would grow without fertilizer. You couldn't live without food, could you?"

"Then if you did all that, why wouldn't your flowers bloom?" Alice asked.

"Oh, that's simple. It wasn't my fault, and it wasn't a question of luck. There just isn't enough sunlight here. This isn't a place for a garden. Look at it."

Alice looked around the back yard. It had

houses on three sides, and a high wall on the fourth. In the very middle stood an immense horse chestnut tree. "You might as well try to grow flowers at the bottom of a well," Mr. Taylor said.

"The sun shines in when there aren't any leaves on the tree, doesn't it?" Alice asked.

"That's right. But it's winter then. Who expects flowers in winter? We get the sun when we don't need it. In summer the leaves are so thick that precious little light gets through to the plants."

"The old horse chestnut tree is greedy, isn't it, Daddy?"

"That it is," said Mr. Taylor with a sigh.

Alice knew what a real garden was like. Every summer she and her brothers Tom and Alec spent a week with an uncle in the country. Up there the sweet wind blew in freely from the fields, and there were no houses or trees to keep the sunlight away from growing things. Birds never stopped singing, and butterflies fluttered over the bright-colored blossoms.

Plenty of sparrows visited the Taylors'

back yard. Once the children had seen a gray squirrel leaping from branch to branch in the horse chestnut tree. But there were no butterflies.

"Couldn't you try just once more, Daddy?" Alice begged.

"It's no use, darling. It would only be a waste of time and money," Mr. Taylor said, stooping to touch the little girl's flushed cheek. "Someday we may have a house in the country. Then we'll have wonderful flowers. You'll see."

He fastened the garage door and turned toward the house. "Wait a minute, Daddy," Alice said, catching him by the sleeve. "If you're not going to plant a garden, maybe I could have a little corner for a garden of my own. Could I? Could I?"

"I don't see why you shouldn't," Mr. Taylor said. "Who knows? . . . Maybe you could make flowers bloom where I couldn't. I guess I haven't got a green thumb . . . Let's see your hand."

Alice held out her hand and her father laid his thumb beside hers. "Just as I thought," he said. "Your thumb is a lot greener than mine. Don't you see it?"

Alice laughed gaily. "Don't be silly, Daddy," she said. "I see that your thumb is bigger than mine. That's all . . . But may I plant a garden this summer?"

"Of course you may. Take the corner you like best."

"Oh, thanks, Daddy, thanks a lot . . . I guess I'll take that corner. It gets the most sunlight." Alice pointed to the angle formed by a neighbor's house and the wall along the rear of the yard. Her father agreed that that was the sunniest spot, though even that was in the shade a good part of the day.

"When can I start, Daddy?" Alice asked. "When do people plant flowers?"

"If I were you, I'd start right away," Mr. Taylor said. "Flowers ought to be planted in the spring, and it's May already."

Alice pulled her father's head down and gave him a big kiss. "Oh, you're so good! I've got the very nicest Daddy in the whole world . . . Now I'm going to begin right away. But what am I going to plant? I haven't any seeds. Have you got anything I could plant?"

"I don't think so," Mr. Taylor said. "But I can't be sure till I look. Maybe there are some seeds left from last year in the garage. Let's take a look."

The two of them — the big man and the little girl — went into the garage. The man turned everything on the top shelf upside down, while the girl stood on tiptoe trying to see what he was doing.

Mr. Taylor talked to himself as he searched. "Now, what have we got here? A package of turnip seeds . . . and a bag of beans . . . a few peas. You don't want them . . . Aha! What have we here? . . . No, that's lettuce, and this is parsley. I'm sorry, darling, but I can't find anything but vegetables. Not a flower in the lot. You do want flowers, don't you?"

"Yes, I only want flowers," Alice said, looking as if she were going to cry. "Now, what can we do?"

"Don't worry, dear," Mr. Taylor said. "You'll go to the store this afternoon with Mommy and buy some seeds. That's what you can do."

8

So Alice went to the store with her mother that afternoon. When she came home she ran to her father waving a slim package of seeds.

"I picked them out myself!" she cried. "It's pansies. Look at the pretty picture."

The picture on the envelope was very pretty indeed. It showed three big pansies—one purple, one yellow, one pale blue. Alice thought they looked a little like people's faces. "Look, they've got noses and eyes and mouths, like people," she said. "This one looks like Tom; this one, like Alec."

She touched the picture with loving fingers and laid it against her cheek. "Do you think

I can grow pansies as pretty as these?" she asked.

Daddy did not think she could, not in that shady yard; but he did not want to discourage her. "Well, you can try," he said. "Now, would you like me to spade up your corner for you?"

"Oh, no, please don't!" Alice said. "I want this to be my very own garden. It wouldn't be, if you helped me."

"All right, all right," Mr. Taylor said. "But I suppose you'll be willing to use my tools. Go ahead."

It was late afternoon by now. The sun had already set behind the high walls. Still, Alice wanted to begin her gardening right away. But at that moment Mrs. Taylor called them all in to supper. "You can wait till morning to plant your seeds," she told Alice.

The little gardener carried her envelope of pansy seeds to bed with her, and fell asleep with it in her fist. She got up very early the next morning. But the sun was up before her, smiling down, round and yellow, through the leaves. The sparrows were up, too, telling everybody how happy they were.

Alice tried the ground in her corner with her foot. She found it was almost as hard as cement. Softening it up was going to be a tough job. Yet she did not intend to let anybody help her. She got Daddy's hoe out of the garage and set to work.

The handle was much too long, almost twice as tall as she was. Once she gave herself a hard knock on the head with it. By holding it down close to the metal part she managed to hack the earth with quick little blows. Hack-hack, knock-knock, bang-bang, she went. But she was small and her arms were weak. She hardly made a dent in the stony ground. She grew tired, and stopped to rest a bit.

Nine-year-old brother Tom stood by and jeered. "Why don't you let the sparrows scratch it up for you?"

"Go away, Tom, and leave me alone," Alice said taking up the hoe again.

"Come on, sparrows," Tom called. "Come

on, sparrows, and help Alice scratch up her garden."

"Won't you go away and be still?" Alice cried, beginning to get angry.

Tom tried to pull the hoe out of her hands. "Come on now, let me do it for you," he said. "Give me the hoe. Give it to me!"

Alice hung on to the hoe handle and shrieked for help. "Mommy, Mommy, look at Tom! Make him let me alone!"

Mrs. Taylor ran out and ordered Tom into the house. As he followed her, he looked back over his shoulder and stuck out his tongue at his sister.

Now Alice was able to finish her work in peace. When it was done there wasn't much to show for all her hacking and digging and scratching. She had stirred up the earth in her corner to a depth of about half an inch. That was a poor beginning for a pansy bed.

Alice was surprised to find so little in the pretty envelope. There were really hundreds of seeds, but they were almost as fine as dust. All together they would not have filled her doll thimble. She scattered them on the loose earth. Then she raked them in and smoothed the surface, as she had seen her father do. And that was the way little Alice planted the pansy bed.

She ran a stick through the envelope with the pretty picture on it, and stuck it in the ground in the center of the bed. It stood straight up, like a flag, to warn people not to walk there, because that was Alice's garden.

After supper Daddy and Alec, Alice's ten-year-old brother, came out to take a look at the tiny garden. Mr. Taylor shook his head and said, "It will be a miracle if a single one of those seeds comes up."

## The First Trial: Tom Is a Bad Boy

*A few days* after Alice planted her pansy bed the children made a playhouse. This was something they did every year. They always had to wait till the frost was out of the ground, and the days were warm enough for them to play outdoors. May was the best month for that.

Their playhouse was a funny one. It had no real walls or roof. It was just a floor, laid out on the ground like a map or picture. The outside walls and the partitions between the rooms were made of white shells and bits of brick.

The house this year was very elegant. It had three rooms — a living room, a kitchen, and a bedroom. Each child had a room. The living room ran across the whole front of the house; the other two rooms, side by side, were in back. Alec, because he was the oldest, had the living room. Tom had the kitchen. The bedroom was left to little Alice. She would have preferred the kitchen. In a kitchen she could play in water and make mud cakes. There wasn't much one could do with a bedroom.

Alec made a truly beautiful living room. He spread a piece of old velvet curtain on the ground for a rug. He made a couch out of a plank and two bricks. He borrowed from Alice two doll chairs and a piano. On an empty paint tin, used as a table, he put several pieces of colored glass and a china dog without a head.

Tom's kitchen was wonderful, too. He had the best things in the whole house. There was an iron stove you could light a real fire in,

and a sink with running water. The sink was
an old dishpan standing on four bricks. The
water ran into it from a rusty oil drum,
through a length of rubber hose. There was
even a cupboard — a plank with a dozen
broken dishes on it.

Alice did the best she could with her bedroom. She spread a faded bath mat on the
floor. She brought down her doll's bed and
carriage, and a red armchair.

While the children were busy building the
house a pair of cardinals flew into the yard.
The male, a flash of pure red among the
leaves, the female in her drab coat, with red
feet and beak.

"They're the very first cardinals to come
into our yard," Alec said.

"We ought to put a ring around the date
on the calendar, and call this 'the day the
cardinals flew in,'" Tom said.

The birds went away as suddenly as they
had come, and the children returned to their
play.

Alice was not satisfied with her room. Alec
had the headless dog, Tom had the stove and

running water. What could she do to make her room as fine as theirs? She had a bright idea. She would invite a guest. She ran into the house and came out carrying Mr. Andrews, the family guinea pig. When Tom saw her put the cage down in her bedroom, he set up a howl.

"That's not your guinea pig, Alice!" he shouted.

"He's as much mine as yours," Alice called back.

"He belongs to all three of us."

"I don't care. I've got him now, and I'm going to keep him. You've got all the other nice things."

"But look at him," Tom said. "He's eating all the time. People don't eat in bedrooms. Mr. Andrews belongs in the kitchen, where the dishes are."

Mr. Andrews was eating. All hunched up in a corner, he was nibbling a lettuce leaf. In fact, he never did anything but eat.

Tom and Alice might have gone on quarreling all day, if Alec had not settled the dispute. "Let Alice keep him," he said. "He's partly mine, too. I give my share to her. That makes two against one." He pushed Tom back into his kitchen.

Then a terrible thing happened. Alice took the guinea pig out of his cage and put him into the bed, all covered up to his furry chin. She forgot that her room did not have a real door or real walls. As soon as her back was turned the guest jumped out of bed and dashed across the yard.

"Help, help!" Alice shouted. "Mr. Andrews has got out!"

They had a hard time catching him. Back and forth across the yard they raced. A dozen times they thought they had him cornered, but he always slipped between their legs. They made more noise than nine pigs under a gate. When they finally did catch the panting little beast, the playhouse was nearly ruined. The clam-shell walls were scattered, the sink was upset and the water was running over the ground. The piano had lost two of its legs.

Tom blamed Alice for bringing the guinea pig out. "It's all your fault," he screamed.

"You had no right to bring Mr. Andrews into the house. You've ruined everything . . . Now see what I'm going to do to you!"

And the boy went over to Alice's pansy bed and stamped up and down on the freshly planted seeds. Alice was furious. She rushed at her brother with such force that she knocked him flat on his back, right on top of a batch of wet mud pies. He was taken by

surprise, and just lay there with the little girl on top of him, pounding him with her fists and crying, "You've killed my pansies! I hate you! I hate you! I wish you were dead!"

Alec separated the angry pair, and held them at arm's length from each other. At that moment Mrs. Taylor hurried out of the house.

"Stop it, stop it right away!" she called.

"I don't know how it started or who's to blame. But Alice, I'm ashamed of you. I never saw anybody in such a temper. And the dreadful things you were shouting. What have you to say for yourself?"

Alice was sobbing so hard she could not say a word, but Alec spoke up for her. "It wasn't Alice's fault, Mommy," he said. "Tom walked on her flower bed."

"What a terrible thing to do!" Mrs. Taylor said. "You shall be punished for this, Tom . . . Still, Alice, you had no right to act as you did. Come into the house with me, both of you."

Alice took her mother's hand, sobbing, "He killed my pansies! I know he did."

And that was the first trial of the pansy bed.

# Two More Trials

*In June* a great flock of sparrows, coming from somewhere or going somewhere, spied the tall horse chestnut tree in the Taylors' back yard. They decided to stop and rest awhile in the leafy branches. Before long hundreds of them had settled on the ground, scratching around for something to eat. They made a terrible noise, all chirping at once.

Alice heard the racket and looked out of her bedroom window. What she saw sent her

flying downstairs and out into the yard. Her garden was covered with birds, and a hundred little feet were digging up the tiny seeds she had planted. She ran toward them, waving her arms and shouting, "Go away, go away, bad sparrows!"

Of course they all flew up into the tree. But they did not stay there. As soon as Alice went away they dropped down on the pansy bed. Again they were driven off. Again they came back. And each time they stole a few more seeds. Oh, the dreadful pests! Were they going to stay in the yard till every last seed was eaten?

Poor Alice wept and howled. Alec and Tom ran to help her. The three children threw sticks and stones into the tree, and Tom beat his drum and roared like a lion. They ended by driving the whole flock out of the tree and the yard. But within the hour they were back again. Then Alec had a bright idea.

"Let's make a scarecrow," he said. "That's how Uncle John frightens the crows away from his corn."

So they made a scarecrow — a very beautiful one. They began with a broomstick. They nailed a shorter stick across it near the top, for shoulders. They fastened two more sticks to the ends of these shoulders, for arms. Then they put one of Daddy's old shirts on it. Having no straw, they fattened it out with newspapers. At the end of the arms they tied a pair of black gloves. They pinned a pair of ragged pants to the bottom of the shirt. Now the good fellow was dressed.

Last, they gave him a head, a basketball with eyes, nose, and mouth painted on it. They finished it off by crowning the head with an old flowered hat that Mommy used to wear. When their scarecrow was set up in the center of the pansy bed it looked so funny that the young artists plumped down on the ground and laughed till their sides hurt.

It kept the sparrows away. At least, none of them came back. Tom said that was not because they were afraid of the scarecrow, but because there were no more seeds for them to eat. Daddy agreed with Tom. He said to Mommy, "I'm sure Alice will never

see a pansy in her garden. To begin with, the earth is too poor, and there isn't sun enough. Then, Tom walked on the bed, and now the sparrows have eaten the seeds. Poor kid!"

That was the second trial of the pansy bed.

Then came the rain. When the first quiet drops began to fall Alice was glad. She said the garden was going to get a good watering. But the rain did not seem to want to stop. For two days it fell harder and harder, till it was pouring down in bucketfuls. A high wind rose, too, and the air grew chilly.

Then Alice began to worry. From her bedroom window she watched the rain pelt down on her beloved pansy bed. It ran in trickles, it ran in streams, washing away the soft earth and the seeds in it.

"There isn't going to be a single seed left," Alice sobbed. Her pretty face was streaked with tears.

"Well, crying won't help things," Tom said. "Isn't there water enough around today, without your adding more to it?"

"Yes, Alice dear," Mommy said. "You can't help your pansies by standing and looking at them. Forget the rain for a minute, and go and play with your brothers."

The boys were playing the game Alice liked best. It was called jackstraws, and was played like this. A handful of colored wooden sticks was dropped in a heap on the table. The players picked up one stick at a time with a wire hook. They took turns. Each one pulled out as many straws as he could without moving the others. When he did move a straw, ever so little, he turned the hook over to another player. The one who had lifted out the most straws at the end of the game was the winner.

But today Alice could not get interested in the game. Her hand shook so that she moved other straws right away. While Alec and Tom were taking their turns, she kept getting up and wandering over to the window. Finally they told her not to come back, because she was slowing up the game.

When Mommy came into the room some time later, she had disappeared. "Where's your sister, boys?" Mommy asked.

The boys looked up from the game. Alec

said, "She was standing at the window, crying as usual. I guess she went to her room."

But she had not gone to her room. She had put on her coat, hat, and boots and slipped outdoors. With head lowered against the pelting rain, she ran to the garage and got her father's hoe. Then across the yard to her garden she dashed. The pansy bed was on a sort of hump in the corner. The water was pouring down this in all directions. What Alice planned to do was to throw up a low bank, or dike, around the bed to keep the seeds from washing away with the earth. This was not a bad idea.

The earth, once so hard, had turned to mud and was easy to move. Round and round the bed Alice went, hoeing up a low bank. It was nasty work, in the wind and rain. Water ran down her neck and got into her eyes and made the hoe handle slippery, but she kept bravely on. Fortunately, no one saw her before she had built a mud wall a few inches high all around the hump. Then she put the hoe back in the garage and stole up to her room, her heart singing with joy because she had saved her pansies.

Now that was the third trial of the pansy bed.

When the rain stopped, Mr. Taylor went out to look around, and saw Alice's little mud wall. He shook his head sadly. "She built it too late," he said. "The rain had already washed all the seeds away." Then he added, "It will be a miracle if a single one comes up."

But, believe it or not, some seeds did come up. It was Alice who saw them first. She got down on her hands and knees a dozen times a day and examined every square inch of the bed. She did not exactly know what she was looking for, as she had never seen a pansy plant. She simply knew that they would be green.

And one day she saw them, a number of tiny, tiny green leaves sprouting out of the ground. Only a few were on the humpy part of the bed. Most of them were in the fine sand that had washed down against the bank. Alice was terribly excited. She called to her

brothers playing in another part of the yard,
"Oh, Alec, Tom, come quick! Come look!
My pansies are up!"

The boys got down on all fours and looked.

"I see something," Alec said. "But it could be grass."

"I think it's weeds," Tom said.

"No, it's pansies. I'm sure it's pansies," Alice cried. "Wait . . . I'll ask Daddy."

Mr. Taylor came and took a good look at the little green sprouts. "Well, well, well!" he said. "I'll be hanged, if they're not pansies! Who would have believed it? . . . Boys, your little sister has a green thumb."

Then they all shouted, "Hurrah for Alice! Hurrah for Alice!" and joined hands and danced around the bed. The little gardener was so happy she cried a little, then laughed a little, then cried a little again. Tom forgot what the excitement was about and sang "Happy birthday to you" at the top of his lungs.

That evening they gave Alice a party. Mommy baked a banana cake, and they lit candles. Alice sat in her father's chair at the head of the table. Mommy put a gilt crown on her curls and said, "Alice Taylor, I crown thee the world's first Pansy Queen."

# The Pansies Suffer Again

*No boy or girl* ever loved a pet more than Alice loved her pansies. She counted the plants: there were sixty-four of them. She hardly left them alone a minute from dawn to dark. She watched them unfold their new leaves, each one larger than the ones before it. She fluttered over them in her pink or blue or yellow dress, like a big butterfly. She brushed dust off them with gentle fingers, and watered them every evening. And the plants thanked her for her care by growing straight and strong and beautiful.

One morning Alice found a small package beside her bowl of oatmeal. "Open it," Tom said, grinning.

There was a magnifying glass in the package. "What's this for?" Alice asked.

"To help you see your pansies better," Tom said. Everybody laughed at the funny look on Alice's face.

"You deserved that, dear," Mommy said. "You really are spending too much time out in the garden."

"Am I hurting anybody?" Alice asked.

"Of course you're not hurting anybody. And I suppose it does give you something to do, now that school's out. It looks funny, that's all."

In spite of what the others thought, Alice did not spend any less time with her pansies. She spent even more time. For now something new was added. Tight little buds were sticking out their green noses among the leaves. The plants were going to bloom. Soon there would be blue, purple, and yellow flowers on them, like the picture on the envelope.

Alice thought the buds were the plants' babies, as puppies and kittens are babies of dogs and cats. "My pansies are going to have little ones!" she cried. Nobody could have been happier than she was.

It was near the middle of June when the buds appeared. At that time every year Mr. Taylor had a two-week vacation. The family always spent those two weeks at the seashore. The children looked forward to this vacation all year, as they looked forward to Christmas.

For two or three days before they set out for the beach, they lived in a great state of excitement. They ran around gathering up buckets and shovels, shrimp nets, fishing rods, bathing suits, bats and balls. They packed and unpacked their suitcases ten times a day. They lay awake till midnight, chattering about the wonderful things they were going to do.

Generally little Alice was the most excited of the three children. But this year she did not seem to take any interest in the preparations. The day before they were to leave for the seashore, Mommy asked her, "Aren't you going to pack your things, dear?"

Alice hung her head and twisted the corner of her dress between her fingers. "Is something the matter?" Mrs. Taylor asked, taking the little girl in her arms.

"I'm not going with you this year, Mommy," Alice whispered.

"Not going!" cried Mommy. "Why, child, what do you mean? You always loved the ocean so."

"I love the ocean, but I can't go this year."

"Why? . . . What's the matter with you? You know we couldn't leave you home alone."

"I just can't leave my pansies!" Alice burst out, beginning to cry.

Her mother did not laugh or scold her, or say, "That's silly." She stroked her hair and told her, "I understand, darling. But there must be something we can do."

"But what, Mommy? I couldn't take them with me, and who would look after them here?"

"Let's see . . . What looking after do they need?"

"They have to be watered every day."

"That's right," Mommy said. "But maybe it'll rain soon."

"It won't rain—ever. And besides, I must be here when the first flowers come out . . . Oh, Mommy, don't make me go with you. The plants would all be dead when we got back."

Mrs. Taylor thought for a moment. Then she said, "I know what we'll do. We'll ask Mrs. Dibbs to look after them."

Mrs. Dibbs was the kind old lady who lived next door. She loved flowers, too, and she and Alice were great friends. The children called her Aunt Tabby. "You can count on her to look after your pansies," Mommy went on, "And she'll be here to welcome the first flowers."

Alice's face brightened. She rubbed the tears off her cheeks and jumped down from her mother's lap. "Oh, Mommy, that's a wonderful idea! Do you think Aunt Tabby would do it?"

"There's only one way to find out," Mrs. Taylor said. "Let's go over and ask her."

They found Mrs. Dibbs at home. She was in her own garden, standing knee-deep in snapdragons, larkspur, and petunias. She was a tiny old lady with a sweet voice, kind eyes, and loving hands.

"Why, of course, child," she told Alice. "I'll be only too happy to look after your lovely pansies. I know how much you think of them, and I promise you I'll not let anything happen to them."

"You'll be sure to water them every day?" Alice asked.

"Every single day . . . even twice a day, if the weather is very hot. Now, run along and have a good time."

"Then I'll go to the seashore!" Alice cried. And right away she began to get her things together. The way she dashed about, you would have thought she was ten little girls. You see, she had to make up for lost time. She was everywhere at once—in the basement, in the attic, in the garage, in dark closets, under her bed. By suppertime she had got all her things together and piled them alongside her brothers' possessions.

They made such a mountain that Mr. Taylor took one look at them and said, "I want to remind you kids that I'm driving a station wagon, not a truck. I'll take what I can, but I'm sure we'll have to leave half this stuff behind."

In the end they managed to get everything in the car. Not a bucket, shovel, ball, bat, fishing rod, shrimp net, bathing suit, bag or box was left behind. While Alec and Tom were helping Father squeeze the things into

the rear of the car, Alice slipped out to take a last look at her pansies. Mrs. Dibbs found her there when she came over to say good-by.

"You really love your pansies, don't you, dear?" she said.

"Oh, I do, I do," Alice said. "Look at the buds. They'll be big flowers when we get back . . . You won't let anything happen to them, will you, Aunt Tabby?"

"I certainly will not. I'll take as good care of them as I would of a sick child. Run along, now, and don't worry."

Alice didn't worry, though not a drop of rain fell in all the time they were at the seashore. It was the very best weather for playing outdoors. Alice saw the earth drying up and turning to dust, but she was sure Mrs. Dibbs would give the pansies plenty of water.

With Alec and Tom she did all the things children usually do at the seashore. They held hands and jumped over the waves. They lay in the sun and got brown. They buried poor Daddy in the sand up to his neck. They built castles which the high tide washed away. They went fishing and caught six slimy eels that wrapped themselves around their arms. They played ball and tennis with other children on the beach. They picked up a basketful of shells. They bought soft drinks and ice cream from the old man who went up and down ringing his little bell.

The days were too short and too few for all the things they wanted to do. Night always came before they had finished their play. Not a drop of rain fell to spoil their fun, and it was very, very hot. Yet Alice did not worry about her garden. Whenever she thought about it, she would say to herself, "Aunt Tabby is giving the pansies all the water they need." You could hear her happy laughter everywhere all day long.

They were all sorry when the day came for them to go back home. Loading the car for the return trip was not fun, as it had been when they were leaving. It was work, and the boys grunted and sweated as they carried their things out. The three children took their places in the station wagon with sad

faces, and nobody laughed or sang during the trip.

As they drew near the city Alice began to fidget. It seemed that she could not wait to see her pansy bed. "Can't you drive faster, Daddy?" she asked two or three times.

She was out and dashing across the yard before the car had come to a complete stop in front of the house. A loud wail coming from the direction of the pansy bed brought the others running toward her. What they saw made them want to howl, too. *The pansy plants were dead!* At least, they looked dead. They were lying flat against the sun-baked earth, their leaves mostly brown or yellow.

"Oh, my poor pansies, my poor pansies!" cried Alice. "They're all dead!"

Brother Alec gave one look at the plants and ran to fill the watering can. The thirsty earth took a deep drink, and still he poured on water till it ran off in all directions.

"That bad old Aunt Tabby didn't water my pansies," Alice sobbed. "She lied to me. She told me to go and she'd take good care of them. She's a bad old woman!"

Mrs. Taylor took the sobbing child in her arms. "You shouldn't talk like that," she said. "There must be some good reason why she failed to water them. Let's go over to her house and find out."

Mommy and Alice went over to Mrs. Dibbs' right away. They did not find her at home, but tacked on the door was a sheet of paper on which the old lady had written:

DEAR ALICE,

I'm terribly sorry that I cannot look after your pansies till you get back. My daughter in Philadelphia is sick and has sent for me. I'm leaving at once. Please forgive me. I hope it rains soon.

Your loving

AUNT TABBY

The note was dated the eighteenth of June, a week after the Taylors left for the seashore. "Then my poor flowers haven't had any water for a whole week!" Alice cried. "No wonder they're dead."

"But Alice dear, you mustn't blame Mrs. Dibbs," Mommy said. "You wouldn't expect her to stay here just to look after your pansies, and let her daughter suffer, would you? And maybe some of the plants will live after all. Maybe Alec watered them in time."

Some of the pansies did live. When Alice came out after supper, in the cool of the evening, she found that about a dozen had revived. The greenest of them were standing straight again, with silver drops of water glistening on their leaves. And there were blooms on them. Some were blue, some yellow, some purple. They had faces, like the flowers in the picture. Alice laughed when she found one that looked like Tom and another that looked like Aunt Tabby.

Now that was the fourth trial of the pansy bed. First, you will remember, Tom walked on it. Second, the sparrows scratched it. Third, the rain drowned it. Fourth, the drought burned it. But nothing could kill little Alice's brave pansies.

Daddy leaned over and gently touched the largest yellow flower. "I don't believe my eyes," he said. "It's a miracle. That's what it is."

## Tom Gets Some Pansies

*The few pansies* that had lived repaid Alice
for her worry and work. Each one of the
dozen plants had several blooms on it. There
were so many the whole bed was covered with
flowers. Alice helped them by loosening the
earth around their roots. That gave them air,
and let the water soak in better, Daddy said.

As soon as Mrs. Dibbs returned she went
over to see Alice. She told her how sorry she

was that she had had to go away. "Did all the pansies die?" she asked.

"Oh, no," Alice said. "A good many of them lived. I don't blame you, really I don't . . . Come out and see them."

She tucked her warm little fist into the old lady's bony hand, and the two of them went out to the garden. Tears came into Mrs. Dibbs' eyes when she looked down on the bright flowers, blue, yellow, and purple, laughing in the sun.

"Oh, aren't they lovely!" she cried. "I've never seen anything like them."

"Pick one, Aunt Tabby," Alice said, which was a sign that she was not angry with her old friend.

Mrs. Dibbs picked a yellow pansy and stuck it in the buttonhole of her jacket. Then she handed Alice a small package wrapped in pretty gift paper. "Here's something I brought back for you," she said. "I think you'll like it. Open it."

Alice removed the wrapping carefully, so as not to tear it. Inside was a pair of small china vases. Alice saw at once why Mrs.

Dibbs had given them to her. They had bright-colored pansies painted all over them.

"They're very old," Mrs. Dibbs explained. "My grandmother painted them when she was a girl — a long time ago."

Alice threw her arms around the old lady's neck. "Oh, thank you, thank you, thank you!" she cried.

"They'll be nice with pansies in them, won't they?" Mrs. Dibbs asked.

"They would, if I dared pick any," Alice said. "That would kill the plants, wouldn't it?"

"Oh dear, no," Mrs. Dibbs told her. "Quite the contrary. You ought to pick flowers, all kinds of flowers. That keeps them blooming. If you leave all the blooms on, the plants will go to seed."

"I didn't know that. I'm glad you told me, for now I can pick some," Alice said. And she set to work at once to make a little bouquet. She did not put the pansies in her vases, but handed them to Aunt Tabby.

"I'll pick some for Mommy tomorrow," she said. "These first ones are for you."

About a week after the Taylors got back from their vacation, Tom fell sick. Mrs. Taylor said he must have picked up some sort of bad virus at the seashore. Alice had no idea what a virus was. She thought it must be something ugly, like a sand crab or a sea worm. Poor Tom complained of a headache, and was sick to his stomach. The doctor came with his black bag. He pounded Tom on the back, felt his pulse, looked at his throat. He stuck a needle into his arm, which made Tom wince. Then he told Mrs. Taylor that the boy should be kept in bed and not given anything to eat.

Alice stayed close to her mother when she went to the door with the doctor. She heard him say, "Tom's a very sick boy. Keep the other children away from him. I'll drop in again tomorrow morning to see how he is."

Alice was frightened. She asked her mother, "Is Tom going to die, Mommy?"

"Oh dear, no," Mommy said. "You must not think of such a thing. But we shall have to keep him quiet. Now run outside, and don't bother me."

Alice tiptoed down the hall and out into the back yard. She went to her pansy bed, as you would go to a good friend for comfort. She sat down beside it and began to cry. Through her tears she saw the beautiful flowers. They were smiling and nodding to her, but she was too miserable to pay any attention to them. She rocked back and forth, saying to herself, "Tom's going to die, I know he is."

Then she remembered what she had said the day Tom walked on the pansies. While she was pounding him she had cried, "I wish you were dead! I wish you were dead!"

It was all her fault, then, if her brother was sick. She had wished he would die, and she was going to get her wish. It wasn't a sand crab or sea worm that was making him suffer. It was her own wicked wish. She was too frightened to breathe.

After a while she went into the house and crept upstairs as softly as a kitten. In front of Tom's door she listened a minute. No sound came from within. She turned the knob, opened the door a little, and peeked in.

There lay Tom, pale and motionless. But he was still breathing. He stirred in his sleep and whimpered, like a puppy.

Alice met her mother in the downstairs hall. "Oh, Mommy," she said. "Tom's awfully sick. Is there anything I can do to help him to get well?"

Mrs. Taylor noticed that her little girl's face was red and swollen with weeping. "Don't take on so, dear," she said. "He'll soon be better. You can help by keeping out of Mommy's way and being quiet. I'll call you if I need you."

Alice went back to the pansy bed. She felt a little angry with the pansies now. Were they not partly to blame for her brother's sickness? If there hadn't been any seeds, Tom wouldn't have walked on them, and she wouldn't have had to make the wicked wish. But wasn't there something they could do together, the pansies and herself? Maybe if she picked the pansies and gave them to Tom he would get well. Anyway, what good would flowers do her, if her brother died?

She stooped over the bed, and when she

straightened up her hands were full of pansies. In her great hurry she had not picked them carefully, one by one, pinching off each flower with a nice long stem. She had torn some off without a stem, and even pulled some up by the roots. Now the bed looked as if a flock of chickens had been playing in it. It was quite ruined.

Back to the house Alice ran. She filled her pretty vases with water and stuck the pansies in them as well as she could. She carried them into Tom's room and put them on the table beside his bed. In so doing she clinked a vase against a glass of water. The sound awoke the sick boy.

"Look, Tom," Alice whispered. "I've brought you some pansies. Now won't you get well — please."

Tom gave one look at the flowers out of a half-closed eye. "That's nice," he said. "Now go away and let me sleep."

The pansy bed never got over that trial. Still, as Daddy said, it was the end of the pansy season. The plants would have stopped

blooming in a few days, if left to themselves.

Of course, Tom got well. Alice always believed that her pansies cured him. And why shouldn't she? She had given him what she loved most. When the bouquets were quite withered, she took the one still-fresh pansy, a big yellow fellow, and pressed it between the pages of her favorite book. In that way she could keep one flower forever.